Weekly Reader Children's Book Club presents

SPROUT

Books by Jenifer Wayne
Sprout's Window Cleaner

SPROUT

Jenifer Wayne
Illustrated by Gail Owens

McGraw-Hill Book Company
New York   St. Louis   San Francisco

Book Design by Marcy J. Katz

Library of Congress Cataloging in Publication Data

Wayne, Jenifer.
  Sprout.

  SUMMARY: A boy with a passion for elephants sets out to buy one,
only to meet with disaster.
  I. Owens, Gail. II. Title.
PZ7.W35128So   [Fic]   75-41341
ISBN 0-07-068695-5 lib. bdg.

Weekly Reader Children's Book Club Edition

SPROUT

You had only to look at the top of his head to see why he was called Sprout. Right from birth, it had been like that. The bit of hair that stuck up was silky and almost white. The nurses in the hospital said they had never seen anything like it. It was one of the nurses who had given him his nickname. His mother was pleased, because she had always had a fear of being handed the wrong baby in such a large hospital, with so many red faces in so many white cribs. But as soon as she saw him, there could be no mistake.

"He's the one with the sprout," she would say firmly to the nurses when they brought the babies into the ward at feeding time.

But Sprout was different from the others in more ways than the top of his head. To begin with, he wouldn't wake up. He had a very short straight nose and a very wide firm mouth, and his eyes were always shut. His eyebrows, if they had been there, would have been raised loftily, as if to say "Please Do Not Disturb." At that stage he had no eyebrows, only faint pink bumps; but he still managed to look as if he thought it was a pity all those other crying babies were there at all. Sprout slept—he never cried.

The trouble was, he never took any feedings, either. Not for a whole week, because he was always sound asleep. The nurses made themselves quite hot and bothered, trying to wake him up. They shook him; they held him upside down; they even took off all his woolly clothes in the hope that a breath of cool air on his body might startle him into crying. But Sprout slept on. His mother worked herself up into a state, worrying that he might starve. The nurses told her they were giving him drops of glucose from time to time.

"He won't starve," they said cheerfully.

He didn't. On the seventh day, he woke up of his own accord; he took one look at the side of his cot and another at the huge pink thing somewhere above it. It was the night nurse's face. It was the first one he had ever seen, and he set up a squall such as the hospital had never heard before.

From then on, he ate and ate and ate. His mother wondered afterwards whether she had overdone the feedings. She had been so anxious for him to catch up on that lost week that she ended by making him what polite people called chubby. Honest ones, such as his father, simply said "He's getting fat."

For just as, at first, nobody could stop Sprout from sleeping, now nobody could stop him from eating. Once awake, he was wide awake; once having tasted food, he was always hungry.

"More in there," were the first words he ever spoke. It was one day when his mother was feeding him his strained baby food out of a cup and had decided that he must surely have had enough. But, as she took the cup away, he craned beady-eyed over the tray of his high chair and said those three accusing words: "More in there." There was no hiding from him anything he really liked; what he didn't like, he wouldn't touch at all. Once he threw a whole plate of prunes and custard against the wall. The stain was there for years.

For Sprout, it was all or nothing. When the Visiting Nurse first came to see him, she took one look, said "My goodness, what character!" and backed away. At that time he was asleep, strapped into his carriage on the roof. They lived in an apartment then, and the roof that jutted out from their landing was the only place for the carriage, which had to be lashed to the chimney with ropes so it wouldn't blow away in a high wind. There were a great many winds that first year, but through them all, and through rain, hail, snow and blizzards, Sprout would sleep on, if that was what he had decided to do. His nose was still straight and his mouth still firm, but he now had the silvery beginnings of eyebrows, and the sprout on top had changed from almost white to almost yellow.

By the time he was three, his hair was like straw. It stuck up stiff and thick and bristly, and no combing, brushing, cutting, soaping, or even pinning would keep it down.

It was when he was three that Sprout was shown his baby sister. They told him she was called Tilly. By this time, of course, he could say a great many other things besides "More in there," but he didn't choose to talk very much. He said what he meant, no more and no less.

So when he was taken to the small back bedroom—they had moved into a house now—and saw the scarlet face yelling in a frilled wicker basket, he looked at it for a moment and then just said:

"I don't like that noise." And he stomped out.

"At least he's honest," his father grinned.

"I do hope he'll be kind to her," his mother worried, "and not rough."

But Sprout really had no time to be kind or unkind, rough or tender. He had too much else to think about. Tilly was there, and that noise just mixed in with the other noises of the day, such as the vacuum cleaner and the whistling kettle. What really mattered were his two great new interests: hiding and elephants.

They both happened by chance. The hiding began one day when he was sitting peacefully under a bed eating an old bun he had found put out for the birds. He knew it would be taken away if he were found with it, so he went where he wouldn't be seen. He didn't mean to hide, only to eat the bun. But it turned out that his mother had been looking for him for a long time, to take him out shopping. When at last she found him, she said "Sprout, you bad boy, why are you hiding like that?"

She wasn't cross, just surprised. She never knew about the bun because he had finished it by that time and was quietly picking the last crumbs out of the carpet and putting them into his father's bedroom slipper. But his mother seemed so much interested by the hiding idea that he thought he would surprise her again. And again, and again.

He discovered that he liked finding small dark places and sitting in them; he liked the different smells. His mother's closet smelled of lavender and his father's of mothballs. The cupboard under the sink smelled of dampness and the one under the stairs of dry cardboard. Spare electric light bulbs were kept in boxes there, and the only time he was ever sorry for hiding was when he sat on one by mistake. As he became more adventurous, he discovered new hiding places, such as the laundry basket in the bathroom, that smelled so sickly-sweet that he hoped they would find him soon.

His mother began to worry about all this hiding. Perhaps it meant that he was unhappy. In fact, he nearly always managed to take something to eat with him, so he was very happy indeed.

The elephants happened at about the same time. An aunt sent him a toy elephant for Christmas, and soon after opening it he saw a real one for the first time, in a circus on television. The real one stood with its four great feet packed close together on a drum;

the toy one had grey felt feet that spread out as soon as you tried to make him stand up at all. He had to spend all his time lying down or leaning against things.

"I expect Auntie made him herself," his mother explained. She didn't want Sprout to be disappointed. He wasn't, he thought both the real and the toy elephant were very nice. And he began to collect elephants.

By the time he was four, he had another felt one, pink; a blue knitted one; a black wooden one; a brass one; a grey one with stuffed feet and a red-and-gold-tasseled saddle; and a bent cardboard one cut off a corn flakes box.

On his fourth birthday, when he was in the bath, a kind visitor called to bring him a late present. She waited in the hall while his mother took it up to him. He opened it, stared, and then said loudly and slowly:

"Oh! *Just* what I didn't want!"

His mother had thought at first that he was going to say the right thing, the opposite, a nice "Just what I wanted." Now she wished she had shut the bathroom door. The visitor couldn't know that all he meant was that it was a pity to have another brass elephant exactly the same as the one he already had. It wasn't that he didn't like it or was ungrateful. He just told the truth. It *was* a pity.

He began to have elephant tea parties. They were

much better than the dolls' tea parties he had once seen a little girl arranging, because elephants ate more. Dolls seemed to eat about one crumb and two raisins each, and a chocolate candy if they were very lucky.

"That wouldn't do for elephants," he said. "That wouldn't even fill their trunks. They have to have a great deal more than that."

"What?" asked the little girl.

"Sandwiches. Buns. Cookies. Jello. Cheese. Sausages. And of course cake," he added, as if a cakeless elephant would be almost as good as dead.

"All that for tea?" The little girl was amazed.

"Oh yes. And an apple afterwards, to clean their teeth. Well, tusks, then."

The little girl paused to think about all of this.

"But who really eats it all?" she asked slowly.

"I do. Well, I really *am* the elephants, so I have to."

It was partly the hiding, and partly the elephants, that made his mother think it would be quite a good thing when he went to school.

"He needs children to play with," she said, "not just elephants."

"It'll probably bring him out," his father said vaguely.

"Yes, out of the garbage can," his mother sighed. "He hid five times today, and that was where he ended up. I know it had been emptied, but—"

"I wondered why he smelled of disinfectant," his father said.

"And Tilly's too young for him yet. He nearly stifled her this afternoon, trying to make her a trunk out of an old sock. Thank goodness it had a hole in it."

"Does Tilly want to be an elephant too, then?"

"Of course not. No baby wants to be anything, except itself."

So as the nearest large school was still rather far away, they decided to start Sprout off at Miss Poddington's.

"Oh," he said when they told him. "Will I get milk there in the morning?"

They said they expected so.

"I want it with two straws," he said firmly. "And one oatmeal cookie and three ginger snaps."

Then he went away to feed the elephants. Nobody knew whether he was pleased at the idea of Miss Poddington's or not. He wouldn't know himself, until he got there.

2

"Can you tie your own shoelaces?" was the first thing anyone asked. It was a girl in a brown dress in the cloakroom.

"No," said Sprout. "Can you?"

"No." And that was the end of that conversation.

Miss Poddington's was only a four-minute tricycle ride from Sprout's house. For the first week, his mother went with him. She pushed Tilly's carriage with one hand and held onto the tricycle with the other. That is, she clutched the metal rod that hooked over the back axle so that a grown-up could prevent anyone from riding at anything but a very boring speed.

On the last day of the week, this rod was missing. Sprout didn't say whether he knew where it was or not; he just kept quiet. When they had looked for a long time, he pointed out that other people at Miss Poddington's tricycled to school without rods. Then he shot off at what he hoped was a hundred miles an hour, with his feet going so fast that they looked more like propellors than feet. His mother got the carriage around the bend in the road just in time to see him disappear between the laurels of Miss Poddington's drive.

After that, and as the whole ride was on the same side of the street, he was allowed to go by himself. He came home by himself too; this seemed to work quite well at first.

Miss Poddington's house was large and made of pale grayish-yellow London brick, with a white front door up three steps and a round brass-handled bell. Inside the front door there was a black-and white-tiled floor and two ferns in pots, then another door with a glass pane. Sprout saw this only once. After the first day, he was shown where he really had to go, around the side of the house and down some much narrower steps that led to the basement cloakroom. Here he was given a peg for his coat.

On the first day, he took the blue knitted elephant because it was the largest and he had decided to give them turns in order of height. The cornflakes one

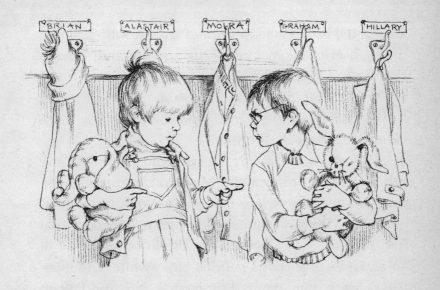

would have to be left out because it was the sixth and
there were only five school days; besides, it was bent.
The blue one was almost too fat to go into the tricycle
basket, but he felt very proud when he squatted it on
the bench in the cloakroom and noticed that another
boy had only a rabbit with a missing eye.

"What's that?" said this other boy.

"My elephant. I've got five more."

"Where are the others, then?"

"At home. Where's his eye?" Sprout pointed at the
rabbit.

"It went down the drain. I was washing him.
Anyway, I had a ride on an elephant once."

Sprout stared. He knew that people did ride real

elephants, but he had never met anyone who had. No one had even taken him to the zoo yet and, for the first time in his life he thought, "It's not fair."

"Your rabbit looks silly," he said.

"So does your elephant," said the other boy. "Besides, elephants aren't blue."

"This one is," said Sprout. He couldn't think of any other answer. Fortunately, Miss Poddington came in then to see if they were ready to go upstairs.

An old lady sat at an upright piano in a room that had brown shiny linoleum on the floor and a lot of small tables and chairs painted pink, white, and blue. There were some painted cupboards, too, and French windows leading out into the garden. Miss Poddington called this room the breakfast room, and she called the old lady Mother.

First they sang "All Things Bright and Beautiful." This took a long time because Miss Poddington had to read out each verse slowly as it came for those who didn't know it. Hardly anybody did, except one very small boy with a pink bow tie who knew all the words but not the tune. He made a queer droning noise that surprised Sprout, but the others seemed quite used to it.

Then some of them had clay, and some had coloring books. Sprout got clay and was just doing an elephant's second ear when Miss Poddington said, "Now anybody who's tired, come to me."

Sprout wasn't at all tired; it was his first clay elephant and it was coming out striped, with thin lines of red, green, yellow, and blue streaking through the gray he had first chosen. This was because other people changed their minds and rolled up cats with bananas, and snakes with eggcups, without bothering to separate the colors. But Sprout liked the stripes and really wanted to stick on this last ear. Still, he really *didn't* want to be left with the boy who had the one-eyed rabbit; and this boy seemed to be the only one not to get up and go to Miss Poddington. So Sprout stood his elephant carefully on a plastic plate, with its ear beside it, and went with the others.

"All right—shall we go and see the pets?" said Miss Poddington cheerfully, and there were twelve squeaks of "Oh yes!"

This meant that two squeaks were missing: one from Sprout and one from the rabbit boy. Sprout kept quiet because he didn't know what Miss Poddington was talking about; the rabbit boy kept quiet because he wasn't listening. He just bent over his coloring book, doing what looked like a lot of purple grass. Everybody seemed quite used to this. Miss Poddington just said, "Now, you'll be all right for ten minutes won't you, Graham?" and left him to it.

They all went through the French windows into the garden. Sprout wondered why anybody would stay indoors drawing purple grass when he could go out on real grass. He wondered even more whether that boy called Graham had really ridden an elephant.

The garden was large and long, with a huge ever-green in the middle of the lawn. It was spring, and there were crocuses growing around the foot of the evergreen, but Sprout wasn't interested in these. He looked up at the tree—dark flat branch above dark flat branch—and thought "I could hide up there." Then he looked at the trunk and thought there was a lot of it before the first branch began. A tall thin person might have swung himself up like a monkey, but Sprout was short and fat. Still, the tree was the best thing at Miss Poddington's so far.

When they came to the end of the garden, Miss Poddington opened a wooden door in a wall. Behind this door was a triangle of rough grass, and on it stood some hutches and boxes with wire netting over the top.

The children rushed forward.

"Can I feed Fluff?" they asked. "Can I stroke Bossy?" "Can we have Marmaduke out on the grass?"

Miss Poddington gave out some lettuce leaves, bread, and bits of carrot. Sprout stood with a piece of bread in his hand and watched while the other children fed the hamsters, the guinea pigs, the rab-bits, and the raccoon.

The girl in the brown dress said she had a guinea pig at home.

"So have I. I've got two," said the small boy with the bow tie.

"I don't believe you," said the girl. "You haven't."

"Well, I'm going to, anyway."

"There you are, you're a fibber. Miss Poddington, Alastair said—"

"I am. I'm going to have them for Easter!" Alastair said loudly.

"Easter's not now; it's not for a long time. Is it, Miss Poddington?"

"Now, Moira, don't let's quarrel," Miss Poddington smiled. "Remember, you're Head Girl this term."

"Only because she's nearly six," muttered Alastair.

Sprout didn't know what a Head Girl was, but if Moira was one, he didn't think much of them. He didn't really think much of guinea pigs either. They were nothing like as nice as elephants.

Miss Poddington turned to him. "Wouldn't you like to give them something?" she asked. "Where's your piece of bread?"

"I ate it," said Sprout.

When they got back to the house, Miss Poddington's mother was there with a tray of small containers of milk. Graham had already started his. It sat on his coloring book with a straw stuck in the top. He had done a lot more purple grass.

Sprout was sorry to see only one straw in each container. He was even sorrier to see that there were no

cookies. Not a sign of one anywhere. But then—
something even worse.

"Where's my elephant?" he said. The plastic plate
was empty. Even the ear was gone.

Graham stared at him. "Why does your hair stick
up like that?" he asked. "It's silly."

"Where's my elephant?" said Sprout.

"Like a big piece of silly straw."

"Graham!" said Miss Poddington. She had only
just overheard this, after giving out the milk. "That's
very rude. You know we don't like rude people here."

Then Sprout saw what was under Graham's coloring book.

"Oh," he said. He was too much surprised to say
anything else.

He picked up the streaky lump of clay. Then he
went very pink, and his sprout of hair stood up more
than ever.

"You've spoiled it!" he shouted at the top of his
voice.

"Graham!" Miss Poddington said. "Well now, that
really was a bad thing to do, wasn't it? That's worse
than just rude, it's unkind. I think you'd better say
you're sorry, don't you?"

Graham scowled.

"Come now, what would you say if Rupert tore up
your coloring book?"

"Who's Rupert?" asked Sprout hopefully.

"You," said Miss Poddington, surprised.

"Oh," said Sprout. Sometimes he quite forgot what his real name was. He was never called Rupert at home.

"He forgot his name!" piped up Moira in the brown dress. "His own name! He *must* be a baby!" And they all giggled.

Sprout stood with his feet apart, very red in the face.

"I know what babies are like," he muttered. "I've got one at home. And it's better than a guinea pig!" he glared at Moira. Suddenly Tilly seemed quite valuable.

"You haven't said you're sorry yet, Graham," said Miss Poddington.

"Sorry," Graham hissed with the purple crayon between his teeth.

"All right, then," she said, "we'll forget all about it."

Sprout was already forgetting; he had suddenly noticed that everybody was eating things. Moira had an apple, Alastair had a bun, and Graham had a big white sandwich. Sprout eyed all these and wondered where they had come from. He marched up to old Mrs. Poddington. After all, it was she who had brought in the milk.

"Are there any cookies?" he asked.

No, she told him, if you want anything to eat you must bring it yourself. She was kind, but quite firm. Sprout looked at the white sandwich and thought, "It's not fair," for the second time. He sipped his milk and watched Graham's jaw moving up and down.

"*Where* did you ride an elephant?" he demanded.

Graham sipped his own milk all the way to the bubbles at the bottom. Then he made a drain-like noise and smiled.

"Oh, somewhere," he said.

"Well, when, then?"

"When I was four."

"What are you now?"

"Five. My rabbit's thirty, though."

"He can't be," said Sprout.

"Yes he can. He was my mother's rabbit," added Graham, as if that made the one-eyed rabbit better than any elephant.

Then the containers were collected, and they had counting and reading, and finished up with the percussion band. Sprout was given a drum, but after one thump he forgot to bother anymore. He was too busy thinking about what he would bring to eat the next day.

His mother asked him what he had done at school.

"Had milk," he said. Then he took a very large spoonful of tapioca pudding and told her through it: "There's a boy there who's *ridden* one."

"Don't speak with your mouth full," she said. "Ridden one what?"

"Elephant," spluttered Sprout. "I want to ride an elephant. When can I?"

His mother said that one day perhaps they would take him to the zoo.

"When? Today?"

"Not today. I can't leave Tilly."

"Tomorrow, then."

"I can't leave Tilly tomorrow, either. Perhaps one day when Mrs. Chad's here."

Mrs. Chad was a very large woman with a very tiny

girl called Albina—pronounced to rhyme with china. Mrs. Chad sometimes came to clean floors and had once or twice minded Sprout and Tilly when their mother had to go out. Sprout liked Mrs. Chad because she cut the bread thick and buttered it heavily and didn't mind how much jam he took. She said she only wished Albina was such a good eater. While Sprout was on his fourth piece, Mrs. Chad was still coaxing Albina through her first.

"Come on, now. A bite for Mom, a bite for baby, and a bite for Mister Elephant. . . ."

Sprout thought all this was silly. He couldn't understand it, but he could easily understand why Albina was so small. She was about half a head shorter than he was and as thin as a pin. Her face was very white and her hair was scraggy, pinned back with a pale blue clip. She never said anything at all, just trailed around after her enormous Mom. Sprout was very much surprised to hear that she was actually eight.

"She shoulda gone to school," Mrs. Chad would say, "but the doctor said not till she fattens up a bit after this 'flu. I tell 'im, I says, if only she could 'ave a bit of my fat. Or yours, come to that," she would add, tickling Sprout in the ribs so that he had to double up and laugh. Tilly, in her high chair, would beam too. Albina simply looked on, with a very blank face and never a sound. Sprout had only spoken to her once, and she had stared at him and not answered, so he didn't bother again. Besides, Mrs. Chad talked all the time anyway.

"When will she come again?" he asked his mother now.

"Perhaps on Tuesday."

"Can I ride an elephant on Tuesday, then?"

But his mother was suddenly occupied with Tilly, who was screaming.

"I don't know; we'll see," was all she said. Sprout's mouth went very tight and straight. "We'll see" was one of the things he most disliked being told. When he was a grown-up, he would *do* things, not just see.

There seemed nothing much else to do now but take an elephant and an apple and go and hide.

"School doesn't seem to have made much difference," said his mother to his father later. She had found Sprout hiding in the grandfather clock.

"Give it a chance," his father said. "He's had only one day."

But Sprout did nothing for the rest of that day but talk about going to the zoo on Tuesday. When he had an idea, it stuck. He told the elephants about it. He even told Tilly, though he felt she understood much less than they did. Tomorrow he would tell Graham, and that Moira.

When it was bedtime, his mother found him stuffing something into a paper bag at the kitchen table.

"What's that?" she said.

"Sandwiches," said Sprout. "White ones. Two."

She looked in the bag and found that there were also four cookies and an apple. Sprout was not going to be outdone again.

3

But when he did tell them at school about the zoo, nobody took much notice. A girl called Sophie had brought a live white mouse, and everyone seemed much more interested in that.

"I'm going to ride an elephant next Tuesday," he told Graham. But Graham only said "Oh."

"I'll have a ride on the biggest one there is," said Sprout. "I might even have two rides. How many rides did you have?"

"Rides on what?" Graham hadn't even been listening. The white mouse had run right up onto his rabbit's threadbare head, and he was the center of an excited circle.

Sprout decided that he might as well go into a corner and eat one of the sandwiches now.

For the rest of that week, it was pets, pets, pets. The white mouse had started something. Every day, somebody brought a different one. There was Moira's guinea pig, and somebody else's goldfish, and a rabbit, and a parrot that could say "Persil washes whiter." Sprout thought this was rather a silly thing to teach any bird to say. "What's for tea?" would have been better, or even just "Hot buttered toast." But by Friday even Alastair had come in with a very small and rather dazed-looking guinea pig. "My mother said I might as well have it before Easter after all," he chirped happily. And all these pets, except the goldfish, had to be taken out to meet the ones in the garden.

Sprout got rather bored. "One elephant," he thought, "would be better than all these pets put together." He became even more bored when Miss Poddington stopped giving him anything to feed them because he always ate it himself.

The only other person who didn't bring a pet to school that week was Graham. But then, Graham had ridden an elephant, so he was all right.

On Monday, even Graham turned up saying that over the weekend he had been to see a puppy, and he was going to have it and would call it Bang. Then Miss Poddington told them all to try to draw their pets.

Graham settled down to do something that looked more like a potato than a puppy; but at any rate it wasn't purple grass. Sprout drew a very good thick elephant, with no erasing. He knew what elephants looked like.

"Well done, Rupert," said Miss Poddington. "Even if it isn't a pet."

Sprout said nothing.

He lived for Tuesday. He had worn his mother into saying: "Yes—if Mrs. Chad turned up; if it wasn't raining; and if Tilly didn't get anything the matter with her before then."

And then when Tuesday came, every one of these things went wrong.

Sprout had hardly been able to last through the morning. He had gulped his milk, gobbled his sandwiches, and shot home on his tricycle. This was the week when he had started to come home alone and his mother had said "Now don't be late. We're going to have an early lunch and go on the bus."

It started to rain just as he rounded the bend of their road. But he didn't take much notice of this. It would probably stop.

But when he got indoors, what should he see but an empty kitchen table (no lunch ready) and what should he hear but wails from upstairs (no Tilly strapped plumply into her high chair) and what should he meet on the stairs but his mother, saying in her most flustered voice:

"I'm sorry, Sprout, but Mrs. Chad rang up to say she can't come. Albina's got a toothache, and now Tilly's broken out in spots. I think I'll have to call the doctor, and I haven't been to the store so lunch'll be a bit late. Anyway, we'll have to go another day."

Sprout stared hard at the bottom stair.

"And it's raining," he said.

"There's a good boy!" smiled his mother, and hugged him. "I knew you'd be sensible!" She hadn't really known anything of the kind; she was just surprised and very much relieved. If she hadn't been so busy, she might have remembered that Sprout was never one to make a fuss. He simply kept quiet and went his own way.

Off she hurried back to Tilly. Sprout stomped out and put his tricycle away in the shed. When he had said it was raining, he hadn't meant to be good; he was just stating the horrid truth. He was too disappointed even to talk to the elephants.

All afternoon it rained. The doctor came and said Tilly didn't have measles, only a food rash.

"So it's all right; we'll go next Tuesday," his mother told Sprout.

She might as well have said "We'll go when you're about thirty-five." Anyway, next Tuesday some other horrid thing might happen.

"What bus were we going on?" Sprout asked later.

"To the zoo? Oh, I think it's a number fifty-three. Why?"

But Sprout had his mouth full of doughnut, and he didn't talk any more that day.

In the morning, he tricycled off with the third tallest elephant and four buns.

"You'll never eat all those buns," said his mother.

"I might give one to somebody else," he said.

She was glad to think that he had found a friend.

About four hours later, she rang up Miss Poddington.

"It's about Sprout—I mean Rupert," she said. "I
was getting a bit worried because he hasn't come
home. Perhaps you had to keep them late? I'm sorry
to bother you, but he's usually home by now."

There was a short silence.

"But he hasn't *been* here," said Miss Poddington.
"He wasn't at school today at all."

4

Sprout tricycled very hard toward the road where the buses went. He thought if he saw a fifty-three bus, he could go on tricycling behind it until it got to the zoo. Or rather, alongside it, he knew he was not allowed to cycle on the road.

He soon saw that this was a silly idea. All the buses were going much too fast for him to keep up with them, especially as he had to try not to mow down the people and dogs and toddlers on the sidewalk. But this didn't stop him. Near the bus stop at High Street was a candy store where the owner knew him. He took his tricycle in there and asked "Please can I park this behind your ice cream thing?"

The man thought he meant for a few minutes. He supposed Sprout's mother must be outside. So he said "Yes, just push it around the back of the refrigerator," and went on pouring mints out of a glass jar.

Sprout took the elephant and the paper bag out of the tricycle basket and walked to the bus stop. There was a line, so he stood in it. He stared very hard at the numbers of all the buses, thinking of the figures in Miss Poddington's sums. When he saw a double decker that he was sure said fifty-three, he got on.

When the conductor came to him, Sprout just said "zoo." He had heard other people ask for places in one word like that.

"Where?" asked the conductor.

"Zoo," shouted Sprout.

"You're goin' the wrong way, son. You want the other side of the road."

So Sprout got off.

He managed to cross through all the traffic and saw a number fifty-three ready to move away in the opposite direction. He jumped onto it just in time, but one of the buns fell out of the paper bag, and sadly he saw it run over by a truck. Never mind, there were still three. He settled down into a corner seat by the door. The conductor was upstairs and didn't notice him for some time. Then, when he came around for the fares, he must have thought that Sprout was with the fat lady in the next seat and had been paid for. It wasn't until later, when the fat lady had gotten off, that this conductor said "Hey—where d'you think you're goin'?" He gave Sprout a rather sour, unhelpful look.

"Zoo," said Sprout firmly.

"That'll be fifteen cents. And don't argue, I saw where you got on."

Sprout didn't argue, he just got off again.

He saw the conductor shouting something as the bus moved away, but it didn't matter. He had only brought thirty cents altogether, and he knew he would need a lot of that when he got to the zoo.

By now, he was in quite a strange place. There seemed to be miles of shops and hundreds of people. He walked in the same direction as the bus until it was out of sight, then he just walked on. And on, and on. There came a place where the road divided in a great fork, with traffic lights and islands and lines of cars slowing down behind each other, three deep and pointing in different directions. Sprout didn't know, now, which of the ways the fifty-three bus had gone. But the roads were so wide and so busy that he decided to stay on the same side of the pavement and hope for the best.

Soon he began to wish he hadn't left his tricycle at the candy store, even though the sidewalk was getting so crowded that he could hardly have wriggled the tricycle through. He had come to a street market. There were stalls piled with fruit and vegetables, combs and necklaces and daffodils, and salted peanuts in bags. Men were shouting everywhere. The gutter was full of cauliflower stalks and squashed tomatoes.

Sprout had a feeling that he was still a long way from the zoo. But he was a long way from home, too. He ate one of the three buns and plodded on.

Just as he came to the end of the market stalls, he stepped right out of one of his shoes. He turned around to pick it up and saw that the lace had broken. There was nothing he could do about this except put the loose shoe on again and try to go on walking with his big toe stuck up like a hook. Soon that leg began to ache, and Sprout's face began to get pinker and squarer, and his sprout of hair began to droop as if it was tired, too.

Suddenly a voice said "Mom! Look!"

It was a small high voice, almost in his ear. He looked around. There, staring straight at him, and pointing, was Albina Chad, with her mother just behind her. Mrs. Chad looked more enormous than ever, in a coat with a big bristly fur collar. Albina looked more pin-like, in a tiny pants suit with a great thick scarf tied around her neck.

"Well!" said Mrs. Chad. "If it isn't him! Mean to say your mother came shopping all the way down 'ere? Where's the baby?" She looked around cheerfully.

"Nowhere," said Sprout.

"He's by himself," said Albina, as she pulled the scarf up around her face. "I saw him come down the road. He's on his own."

It was the first time Sprout had ever heard her speak. He was partly sorry and partly pleased that she had seen him. He certainly was tired, but he still wanted to go where he was going.

"Is this the way to the zoo?" he asked Mrs. Chad.

She gaped at him. "You don't mean to say . . ." she began. Then she looked at the paper bag, and the elephant, and the broken shoelace. "Does your Mom know where you are?" she said.

"No," said Sprout.

"You've run away!" piped Albina.

"I haven't," said Sprout.

"You're lost, then."

"I'm not," Sprout stared squarely at Albina, and she stared pointedly back.

"Whatever you are or whatever you've done, you shouldn't have, that I'm sure," said Mrs. Chad very firmly. "Your poor mother, what must she think? She'll be dead worried about you. Got the police out, I shouldn't wonder. I'll have to go and call her, right this minute. There, and we was just on our way to the dentist."

"I don't wanna go to the dentist, Mom!" wailed Albina.

"Don't be silly, it won't hurt."

"It will. Can't we take him back home instead?" Albina looked at Sprout almost brightly over the top of the scarf. She saw him as a way out of trouble.

"Not before I've called," said Mrs. Chad. "She'll be worried stiff. But I don't want you standin' about with that tooth. Next thing, you'll get a cold in it. You take him back indoors for a minute. Go on, while I run down to the phone booth."

And she hustled Albina and Sprout into a house with front railings right on the pavement and a front door that opened into a passage so dark that Sprout stood feeling blinded. But Albina went straight ahead through another door and into a small room where there were a great many ornaments and potted plants, flowered wallpaper and cushions, and a very big television set.

"Can we turn it on, Mom?" asked Albina.

"Don't you go touching anything electric while I'm gone. You just keep an eye on *him*," said Mrs. Chad. "I don't like leaving the pair of you on your own, but I don't see what else I can do, you with that tooth. And it's past dinner time, she'll be worryin' 'erself silly. Anyway, I won't be long; you just wait quiet, the two

of you. And if anybody knocks at the door, don't
answer!" she added to Albina as she went out.

Sprout stood looking square and pink and miserable.

"It's all gone wrong," he said.

"All what?" asked Albina.

Sprout didn't answer. It was one of the very few
times in his life when he felt like crying. He had
hardly ever done that since he was a baby, and he
certainly wasn't going to do it in front of Albina.

"You didn't run away, and you weren't lost," said
Albina slowly, staring at him. "Then you must've
been goin' somewhere."

"I was. I told you."

"What, when you asked Mom is this the way to the
zoo?"

"Yes," said Sprout. He suddenly felt that Albina
really was older; she looked at him with such a pitying
stare.

"You're dumb!" she said.

"Why am I? I'm not!" He was surprised at Albina's
talking to him like that. He was surprised at her
talking at all. She seemed quite different in her own
home.

"Well, the zoo's miles away. I went once; I was sick
on the bus. The pet shop down the road's better. It's

only a walk, and you can see them right close up. Once he let me hold a rabbit."

"I don't want rabbits," said Sprout.

"There's not only rabbits; there's dogs and kittens and mice and fish and all other sorts of animals—"

"They're just what I don't want," said Sprout. "Anyway, I bet he hasn't got *all* sorts."

"He's got monkeys, so there!" said Albina.

"I don't want a monkey."

"All right, what *do* you want, then? Lions and tigers, I don't see anything *in* them. All they do is walk up and down."

"Elephants don't," said Sprout. He couldn't hold out any longer.

"Oh, *them*," said Albina. "They're too big. My Dad wanted me to 'ave a ride on one, but I wouldn't."

"I would," said Sprout. He looked more miserable than ever. Imagine a person actually refusing an elephant ride! Suddenly he very much wanted to put Albina in her place.

"They're not too big for me," he said. "I wasn't going to only ride one, I was going to perhaps *have* one!" His great secret was out. He stood there, very red in the face, with his sprout of hair looking as if it said "So there!"

"Have one?" repeated Albina. "What, a real live elephant?"

"Yes. I brought my money. I was going to ask how much they cost."

Albina looked at him for a moment with her mouth open. Then, for the very first time, he saw her grin.

"You silly boy!" she said, as if she were old enough to be his mother. "People can't have real elephants! Where would you keep it?"

"In the garden," muttered Sprout.

"You're a great big baby," said Albina. "It'd die!"

These two remarks, on top of everything else, were really too much for Sprout. However hard he didn't want it to, a tear ran down each cheek. He would have given himself away just as much if he had tried to stop them because he had the third tallest elephant under one arm and the buns under the other, and his handkerchief was in the pocket on the seat of his jeans.

And anyway, Sprout was what he had always been: an all-or-nothing person. He never just half cried; either he didn't cry at all, which was the most usual thing, or he cried loudly and a lot. This was what he started to do now, to Albina's great surprise.

"Don't be silly," she said at first, "we'll take you back home."

Sprout cried more loudly.

"I'll get you a butterscotch," said Albina, "I know where they are. Or would you rather have a bun? Mom bought some buns for our tea. Listen, when I went to the zoo, Dad got me a bun to give to the elephant, but—"

Sprout howled.

"Stop it!" said Albina. She was getting rather frightened. "Shut up, can't you? My Mom'll give me what for if she comes back and finds you like that. She'll say it's my fault. Wipe your face, you're all wet. She'll be back in a minute—oh, BE QUIET!" she yelled through the din.

Sprout stopped as suddenly as he had begun. He had no idea Albina could yell.

"Anyway, I've *got* buns," he said. "All I wanted was the elephant."

"What's that under your arm, then?" asked Albina.

"Too small," said Sprout. "I wanted a *real* elephant. Why would it die?" he demanded. "I'd feed it."

"Elephants come from hot countries," said Albina. "It'd be cruel."

The idea of being cruel to an elephant made Sprout look as if he was going to cry again, which was more than Albina could stand.

"Listen," she said quickly, "I know where there's a big elephant, one that wouldn't die, and the man might let you have it. It's been there for a long time."

"Where?" Sprout blinked.

"Down in the junk shop, on the corner. Come on, I'll take you to see it if you like. We wouldn't be gone a minute. Quick, before Mom comes back!"

"Anything to cheer Sprout up," Albina thought. She had never seen him all wet like that before, just as he had never seen her so lively.

"What's a junk shop?" asked Sprout as they hurried down the road.

"That is." Albina stopped and pointed to a corner on the other side of the street, where there were some old red velvet chairs standing out on the sidewalk.

"Where's the elephant?" said Sprout.

Albina grabbed his hand and dragged him across the road. A truck honked and had to swerve to avoid them.

"There!" she said. They stood in an open doorway, looking into a very dark shop. To one side of the doorway was a pile of grubby books and magazines with a bird cage on top. To the other side was a box of mixed china and a black satin dress hanging on a coat hanger. The inside of the shop was so black and so full that, at first, Sprout couldn't make out anything. Then he saw what Albina was pointing at.

Just inside the doorway was a table covered with china and glass. One end of the table was held up by a huge dusty leather trunk, standing on its end. But

under the other end of the table—Sprout gaped—was
the biggest elephant, except a real one, that he had
ever seen.

"It's even as big as a real *baby* elephant," he said.

"I told you so, didn't I?" said Albina triumphantly.
"I told you it was a big one."

"It's red," said Sprout. "I've never seen a red
elephant."

"Well, you have now."

"It's smiling." Sprout was halfway under the table,
looking at the elephant's face. "Why does it have to

have all those things on its back?" he said when he came out again.

"Ask the man," shrugged Albina. "I told you, it's been there years and years."

"Poor elephant," said Sprout. He gazed at it with wonder and pity. Even if it was red and not real, it was so big that it seemed nearer to a real one than any he had ever seen before.

"Now then," said a sudden voice behind him, "everything on that table, twenty-five cents each." Sprout looked up. An old man with glasses, a green eyeshade, and a very dirty jacket was peering down at him. "A quarter," said the man, "anything off of there. What were you looking for?"

"An elephant," said Sprout.

The man shook his head. "No elephants," he said. "There's a china kitten there somewhere. I was going to stick his tail on. You can have him for a nickel if you like. Half price," he explained, as Sprout showed no sign of interest.

"The elephant," said Sprout.

"I did have a plaster squirrel till yesterday, but it was sold. What about the Three Wise Monkeys?"

"How much is the elephant?" Sprout asked.

The man scratched his head. "What're you talkin' about?" he said. "Is this a game or somethin'?"

"Under the table!" squeaked Albina impatiently.

"That's what he wants, the elephant under the table!"

The man pushed back his eyeshade and bent down.

"Well, blow me down!" he said. "Tell you the truth, I'd clean forgotten about him. That table's been standing there so long—"

"Quick, what'll you take for him?" said Albina. She was getting worried in case her Mom was back.

"I've got thirty cents," said Sprout. "You can have it all." The idea of that great red smiling elephant being actually forgotten really made him angry. And with all those things on its back, too. He took his money out of the handkerchief in his seat pocket and banged it down on the table.

"There you are," he said. "Now give me the elephant."

"Wait a minute." The man scratched his head more than ever. "I never said I wanted to sell him, did I? Double of the one over the old Elephant and Castle, he is. I dare say there's a story behind him. I dare say he's well on the way to being a collector's piece. I dare say if you was to ask an expert what he's worth—"

"Can we get him out?" said Sprout. He didn't know what the man was talking about and didn't care. He was more and more determined to have the elephant.

But Albina had been listening with her eyes fixed on the man's face.

"Poppycock!" she burst out suddenly. "In my eye!

You never even knew he was there. You'd forgotten all about him. You never would have thought anything of him if you hadn't seen that money. And you're not getting that either," she squeaked, with her hand slapped over Sprout's thirty cents, "not till you give us the elephant."

The man looked at her, and then at Sprout, and then back at Albina.

"You're some pair, you are," he said with a kind of admiring surprise. "But listen, if I was to let you take the elephant, what about my table? Who's going to hold that up, then?"

"Haven't you got another trunk?" said Albina. She looked anxiously around. "Go on, there's one over there, in that corner, underneath all those fenders. I'll hold the table," she said to Sprout, "while you shove the elephant out and the man goes to get the trunk. Well, get a move on, we don't want to be here all day!"

And before the man could say anything, she had taken hold of the end of the table, and Sprout had dived underneath and come out, elephant first, just as Mrs. Chad appeared on the street corner.

From behind the elephant, Sprout could see that Mrs. Chad looked very upset indeed. Her hair was coming undone, she was out of breath, and her face was red.

"Albina!" she shrieked. "Wherever have you been? I got back home, nobody there, the door wide open, I was frightened out of my mind! If it hadn't been for Mrs. Jones next door, she saw you cross the road— and what d'you think you're doin', I'd like to know!"

"Holding up this table," said Albina. Her face looked pinched. Her stick-like arms were beginning to ache already.

Sprout kept well behind the elephant. His main thought was that he had got it and it seemed a useful thing to have at the moment between himself and Mrs. Chad.

But she had seen him. "And imagine your poor Mom," she said, "what she would say, as if it wasn't bad enough what you done this morning." She turned on Albina again, "But it's your fault. You're old enough to know better. And put that table down this minute!"

"I can't," whimpered Albina rather faintly.

"She's instead of the elephant," said Sprout.

"You're coming back with me, the two of you," said Mrs. Chad. "I've had enough of this. Albina! Let go of that thing and come!"

"But if I let go—" began Albina.

"Everything on that table, a quarter each," said a voice in Mrs. Chad's ear. "Four to six dollars worth of stuff there."

"What do you mean?" Mrs. Chad stormed at the man. "Makin' a poor little child stand there like that!"

"I never made her. I was just—"

"She might harm herself. Where's a policeman, then? I'd like a policeman to see this!"

"I was just looking for a trunk to hold up the other end, but—"

"Hold it up yourself!" bellowed Mrs. Chad, snatching Albina away. The man just caught the edge of the table in time to prevent a landslide of china and glass.

They left him standing there.

"Hey!" he called after them. But Sprout was too busy finding the best way to get the great red elephant along the sidewalk; Mrs. Chad was too much taken up with scolding Albina and re-winding the scarf around her face; and Albina was very soon too tightly muffled to say anything in answer to the man's "Hey." So they just left him there shouting it and holding the table.

When Mrs. Chad had finished with Albina, she started on Sprout. He had managed to pull the elephant to the edge of the curb, ready to cross. He found it best to pull the elephant by its trunk. Pushed from behind, it fell forward and he could see that it might break a tusk. It seemed to be made of plaster, hollow in the middle but still quite heavy. Its head came just on a level with Sprout's.

"You just take that thing back to the man," said Mrs. Chad.

"No," said Sprout. He couldn't believe she meant anything so silly.

"Don't be a bad boy, now. Take it back. Or if it's too heavy, I will."

"Leave my elephant alone!" shouted Sprout as Mrs. Chad moved toward him. "He's mine! I paid for him! I paid all my money!"

"Left it on the table," came a woolly noise from inside the scarf.

"I don't know what you're talking about," said Mrs. Chad, "but I do know this: I just promised his Mom I'd take him home. She can't come down herself, she's got the baby to see to. So I said I'd take him. But I never said I'd take an elephant. You're balmy. How d'you think you're going to get that on the bus? Go on, take it back," she said to Sprout in a more anxious, coaxing way. "There's a good boy."

"I suppose I'll just have to walk," sighed Sprout. He pulled the elephant's front legs down into the gutter.

"Don't be silly," said Albina, "He might get chipped."

Sprout stood and thought. "His feet might," he agreed.

"Walk?" said Mrs. Chad. "Do you want to end up

dead, on top of everything else? *Walk* all that way?"
She looked really shocked.

Suddenly the elephant's feet were in real danger. A
truck pulled up a couple of inches away from them.
Now it was Sprout who shouted "Hey!"

The truck driver jumped out and said "You better
look where you're going, young man."

"I was," said Sprout. Then the driver, who was a
young man with sideburns and a cap, heard the other
"Heys" coming from the junk shop. He looked
around and saw the owner, gray and openmouthed,
holding up one end of the loaded table. The young
man's face split into a huge grin.

"Well, look at Dad!" he said. "What does he think
he's up to? What's the matter, Dad?" He crossed the
pavement to the shop. "Looks like you're stuck for the
day, eh?" He roared with laughter. The junk shop
man nodded angrily at the table and said something;
then the young man went into the shop.

Sprout looked at the truck. Its back was half open,
tied up with old rope; inside, there seemed to be a lot
more old furniture and odds and ends like the things
in the shop.

"We could go home in that," said Sprout.

"Oh, come on," said Mrs. Chad. "We'll never get
anywhere at this rate." She was thoroughly flustered.
"Best leave that thing there," she said with a hopeless
glance at the elephant.

"Mind him for a minute, please," Sprout said to Albina, and marched back to the shop. Mrs. Chad was too dazed to stop him.

Sprout found the young man with the sideburns "walking" a trunk on its end through the maze of junk.

"Lucky for you I came." He was grinning to the man with the table. "Very funny you looked, standing there! What happened?"

"He took the elephant," mumbled the junk shop man. He glared at Sprout.

"What, stole old Flatfeet?" The young man looked at Sprout with surprise and another grin.

"I didn't say he stole it," said the old man. As soon as the trunk was under the table and his arms were free, he pounced on the thirty cents.

"That was all I had," said Sprout, "but I don't mind. Can you take us home?"

The young man pushed back his cap. "Mean to say you *bought* old Flatfeet?"

"His name's Market," said Sprout. He had just thought of it that minute. "And Mrs. Chad says it's too far to walk, so can you take us?"

"Walk where?" The young man was completely puzzled.

"Nobody's walking nowhere," Mrs. Chad burst in. "You come along with me," she said to Sprout "before Albina gets into any more trouble. Well what will people think, seeing her standing there with somebody else's elephant? Kids! I don't know what's come over them!" She rolled up her eyes.

"He could go in the truck," said Sprout, "with me and Albina. Even you might get in," he added to Mrs. Chad, "if it's a strong truck."

The young man in the cap looked at Mrs. Chad's enormous figure and grinned fit to split.

"You're quite a lad, you are," he said to Sprout. "Not exactly bashful, are you?"

"*Is* it strong?" asked Sprout.

"You joking? Carry near on a ton, that truck will."

"That's all right, then," Sprout said cheerfully to Mrs. Chad, and he went out to tell Albina.

"If you asked me why I was doing this, I couldn't answer you," said the young man to Mrs. Chad. They were rattling along the main road, with Mrs. Chad sitting in the front next to him so that she could tell him the way. Sprout and Albina and the elephant were in the back.

"What about me, then?" said Mrs. Chad. "If you'd told me this mornin' I'd be ridin' along in a thing like this—well! And all we was doin' was just goin' to the dentist. Talk about surprises!"

"I never rode in a truck before," Albina was saying to Sprout inside. "I never thought he'd really take us. What will your Mom say?"

Sprout's mother was certainly surprised when the truck pulled up outside the house. But she was so glad to see Sprout back that she didn't much mind how he had come. She asked Mrs. Chad and Albina and the young man in for a cup of tea.

"Hey, what about Market?" said Sprout.

His mother was even more surprised when the young man lifted down the red elephant.

"Where on earth did you get that?" she asked.

"A shop. But the market was there, so that's his name," said Sprout.

He was the only person who wasn't at all surprised. He was just very glad that he had found such a big elephant and a truck that had come exactly at the right time to bring it home.

"Tomorrow I shall take him to school," he said. "Now he can have these two buns."

Market also ate four cheese sandwiches, a boiled egg, a banana, a bowl of shredded wheat, and nearly a whole box of crackers.

"I didn't have any lunch," Sprout explained.

5

It was no good their telling Sprout he couldn't take
Market to school. He just kept asking "Why not?"

"He's too big," they said.

"Nearly as big as a real one," agreed Sprout happily.

"Well, then . . ." they tried to reason with him.

"He'll be the biggest thing of anybody's. Silly old
rabbits, silly old mice. Wait till they see Market!"

"But you can't carry him," his mother said, "and if
you think I'm going to push him in the carriage—"

"I'll pull him," said Sprout, "by the trunk."

"What, all the way to school and all the way back?
Don't be silly."

"Why not?" said Sprout. So they were back where
they started.

But the word "carriage" gave his father an idea. "It's no good," he mumbled so that Sprout couldn't hear. "You'll never get him to school without that elephant. Besides, he hasn't even got the tricycle now. Too late to go for it; the candy store'll be closed." Then he told Sprout to help him carry Market out to the garage.

An hour later, they all came back.

"Market's got wheels!" Sprout beamed at his mother. "Look!"

He pushed the elephant through the back door and it rolled straight across to the refrigerator. Sprout rushed to get there first. "He might chip his tusks," he said. "He's not used to wheels yet."

"Good thing I keep all our junk," said his father. "They're off that old carriage of Sprout's."

Sprout's first carriage had been a secondhand one, bought for use more than for looks. Tilly had a new carriage, pale gray with a cream-colored hood. Sprout had never had a hood; he had never seemed to be that kind of baby.

"So now he can *roll* to school," said Sprout contentedly. "And people can have rides. And I'll laugh."

"Why will you do that?" his mother asked.

"You can't have rides on mice and rabbits. You can't have rides on any of their pets. He'll need a lot to eat," he added, "won't you, Market?"

"But Miss Poddington . . ." began his mother.

"He says Yes," said Sprout, "a lot."

In the morning, his mother went to school with him again. After what had happened she was taking no risks.

"And I'll come and meet you afterward," she said.

"All right," said Sprout. He was so proud of Market that he didn't care what she did. Tied around Market's neck was a bag of cookies and peanut butter sandwiches. In Sprout's side pocket was an apple, and in his seat pocket a bag of peanuts. The sun was shining, Market was smiling, and Sprout was very happy indeed.

As soon as he met Graham, things started to go wrong.

"I've got my puppy," said Graham. "I got him yesterday after school."

He was so excited about this news that he didn't even seem to notice Market, whose wheels Sprout was just bumping down the cloakroom steps.

"I got this," said Sprout. "He's nearly real-sized. Look!"

But Graham hardly looked at all. He was hopping up and down, quite unlike his usual self, and saying "Bang! Bang! Bang!"

"He's got wheels," said Sprout. "You can have a ride on him if you like." He hadn't been going to let Graham ride Market till last because Graham had already ridden one elephant; but he was bursting with pride and longing to have Market admired.

"That's his name, Bang," said Graham, "and he

nearly knows it already. I keep on saying it, and he's going to have a collar with his name on it."

"*His* name's Market," Sprout began, but Graham had disappeared without even looking. Sprout heard him rushing up the stairs shouting "Miss Poddington, Miss Poddington, I've got Bang!" He had even forgotten the one-eyed rabbit; it sat there alone on the bench with drooping ears. Sprout felt quite sorry for it.

But he felt much sorrier when Miss Poddington said, "No, he could not take Market into the schoolroom."

"He's much too big," she said firmly when she found Sprout trying to lug him up the stairs. She had heard, from Sprout's mother, something about yesterday and had decided that Sprout must not be allowed to feel too pleased with himself. Besides, Market's wheels were dripping oil on the carpet.

"Suppose everybody wanted to bring in a great big elephant?" she said briskly. "We shouldn't be able to move!"

"Not everybody's got one," said Sprout. "So not everybody could bring one in."

But all the same, he had to bump Market down the stairs again, back through the cloakroom, up those other steps, and around the back of the house to the outside of the French window where Miss Poddington said Market could stand. Sprout placed him where he could keep an eye on him all the time.

The other children were much more interested in Market than Graham had been, but this wasn't altogether a good thing, either. Miss Poddington thought they were *too* much interested. They kept asking questions:

"When can we have a ride?"

"Why is he red?"

"Can I go first?"

"Can two go at a time?"

"Why is he called Market?"

And when they weren't asking questions, they kept looking out of the French window instead of getting on with their basket weaving.

"Really," said Miss Poddington, "Graham's the only one who's settled down to anything this morning. Anybody'd think you'd never seen an elephant before."

Sprout had never heard her sound cross before, either. He couldn't understand it, because from the way the other children talked, you would think Market was more Miss Poddington's elephant than his. She ought to have been pleased. To make sure that she was, he went up to her and said:

"You can have first turn."

But this didn't please her, either, because it made Moira giggle, and that set everyone else off. They all pranced around saying "Do take a turn, Miss Poddington! We'll push you—do take a turn." Miss Poddington tried to stay firm and bright and smiling, but in the end she became really irritable and told them they were all being rather silly this morning. Sprout thought so, too. For one thing, he didn't see anything funny in the idea of Miss Poddington's taking a turn on Market; and for another, he was determined that if anybody did any pushing, it should be him. The fact that Market was his seemed to be a thing that none of them properly understood at all. They just behaved as if Market was a new school toy. The only one who didn't jump around and giggle was Graham, who sat solemnly trying to make a clay puppy and getting more and more annoyed because every time he stood it up, its legs came off.

"Its body's too fat," remarked Sprout. "Only an elephant can have such a fat body and still stand up. Because its legs are fat, too."

"Bang's legs are thin," said Graham.

"Then you'd better give him a thin body."

"I don't want to."

So that was that. Sprout wondered when old Mrs. Poddington would bring in the milk. He had left the bag of peanut butter sandwiches tied around Market's neck, and that was on the other side of the French window.

Suddenly Miss Poddington said: "Oh dear, I can see we won't have any peace until you've all had your elephant rides. You'd better go out now." She was thinking that it was nearly milk-time anyway and that

Market would be a half-hour's wonder. The novelty would soon wear off. Until it had, they would go on being restless and silly.

As soon as the French windows were opened, Market was surrounded by a swarm of children. Three of them got on his back; another three tried to push him or pull him; the others shouted and squeaked and jumped up and down and bombarded Miss Poddington with remarks like: "You said me first!" "It's not fair!" "He pushed!" and "Look, Alastair's falling off!"

No one said anything to Sprout at all. Suddenly he saw red. Not only Market's red, but the red of rage.

Miss Poddington was trying to talk above the excitement: "Now children, steady; don't be silly; one at a time, and I think you ought to ask Rupert first, don't you?"

But all this, and everything else, was drowned by Sprout's bellow.

"STOP THAT!" he yelled. It was just how Albina had yelled to him, the day before, only much louder. And they stopped.

"He's *my* elephant," said Sprout in the silence. "He wants his sandwiches."

"Well, it's not quite time," said Miss Poddington, "that's why I thought—"

"He wants them now," said Sprout.

One by one the children began to protest.

"Oh but Miss Poddington, you said—"

"You promised—"

"You told us we could have a ride before the milk—"

"As a matter of fact," murmured old Mrs. Poddington in her daughter's ear, "the milkman hasn't come yet. He's late today, so—"

"Market's very hungry," said Sprout.

"Well now," Miss Poddington said brightly, "suppose Rupert lets some of you have a ride now and some later on; how would that be? Only you must let Rupert decide," she added. "After all, it's his elephant. That's only fair. Now, Rupert, who will go first? Not me," she put in hastily, "I think I'm too big."

"What about the sandwiches?" said Sprout.

"Well, let's arrange one ride first, shall we, and then perhaps the milk will have come, and Market will have a still better appetite after his little bit of exercise?"

Sprout stared at Miss Poddington. He thought she was rather silly to talk like that. It was one thing for him to say Market was hungry; it was quite another thing for a grown-up person to go on about it. His mother would simply have said "You can't have those sandwiches yet." Miss Poddington was treating him like a baby.

"All right," he said, "the person who can have first turn is Graham."

Then they all gasped and squeaked and protested.

"But Graham didn't even ask!"

"He doesn't even want to!"

"He hasn't even come out!"

Graham was still sitting in the schoolroom making clay legs.

"Him first," said Sprout.

"But it's not fair!" they grumbled.

"It's my elephant," said Sprout again. "And if he can't go first, nobody can." It wasn't that he liked Graham; he was just fed up with all the others. And Miss Poddington would have to do what he said, too.

In the next few minutes, Graham found himself hustled away from his clay puppy and onto the back of Market. He looked very sulky.

"I don't want to," he said. "I've ridden a real elephant."

"If you don't go," they told him, "none of us can. *He* said so." They looked crossly at Sprout, who took no notice. He was busy getting Market ready to set off, with Graham's feet tucked underneath so that they wouldn't chip the plaster.

"Ready, get set, go!" he said, and gave Market's seat a fierce push. Graham rolled slowly down the slope of the path towards the lawn.

"Doesn't he go well!" said Sprout.

"No," said Graham.

"Why not?"

"He's too slow."

"He goes much faster than this without a person on. Look, he can go quite fast even *with* one." Sprout pushed harder, puffing.

"I don't call that fast," said Graham. "You should see Bang."

"He can go faster than this," Sprout panted. He pushed harder still.

"Not like Bang."

"All right—wait till we get back on the path—" Sprout heaved for all he was worth. He knew that the carriage wheels would run quicker on the hard gravel than on the soft grass.

"Bang goes like the wind," said Graham.

"So does Market," gasped Sprout.

"He doesn't. No elephant does. No silly elephant could go as fast as—"

"You just wait and see! You just—*there*!" Sprout had reached the gravel, and he gave the biggest push of all—so big that he lost his hold on Market's seat and fell flat on his face.

But this was nothing to what Market did. The wheels shot forward. There was a bend in the path. Graham held tight and saw a lawn mower rushing toward him.

There was a crash. A second later, Graham was sitting in a flower bed; but Market was rammed against the mower with his feet and wheels in the air.

"I told you he could go fast," began Sprout as he picked himself up. "Elephants are just as fast as—" Then he saw.

On the gravel beside the lawn mower lay a red plaster trunk.

"Well," said Miss Poddington, "at least nobody seems to have come to any harm." She had brushed

the dirt off Graham's trousers and the gravel off Sprout's knees. "It's a good thing you were wearing jeans," she remarked cheerfully. "What a shame about his trunk," she went on, "but never mind, I expect it can be mended. Anyway, I believe the milk's here now, so let's all go in, shall we? Feeling all right, Graham? That *was* a nasty bump, wasn't it?"

They all looked at Graham with interest and began to trail into the schoolroom where Mrs. Poddington had the containers ready. They seemed to have given up any idea of even wanting to ride an elephant without a trunk.

"If I were you I should take him around to the side by the cloakroom for the rest of the morning," Miss Poddington said to Sprout. "Then he can't have any more accidents, can he?"

"He's just got a stump now," said Moira.

"He didn't look where he was going," Alastair remarked primly. "It's a pity."

Sprout stood there with the trunk in one hand. He couldn't believe it. But he had to. A few minutes ago, Market had been a beautiful big smiling red elephant. Now there was just the smile, and above it a round white plaster snout. It was the worst thing that could have happened to any elephant. Sprout was sure that mending would be no good. He was too dazed to say anything or do anything. He just stood there.

"Well, go along," said Miss Poddington kindly but briskly. "And then come and have your milk."

Sprout began to push Market slowly away. As he went, he heard Moira say: "D'you know what it looks more like? It looks more like a pig now!" And they all laughed.

Suddenly he decided what to do. He looked around the garden. Where would be the best place? Of course, there was that one place he had thought of on the first morning and had always thought of again, every time he passed the evergreen. If only the bottom branch were not quite so high off the ground. . . . Then he looked at Market again and didn't have to look any farther.

He pulled the wheels sideways to the tree so that they couldn't run away. There were roots sticking up out of the grass at each end. He laid the broken-off red trunk carefully down by the crocuses. Then he took off Market's string collar, with the paper bag on it, and put it around his own neck. There was no need to make himself even more miserable by hiding without food. Then he climbed up onto Market's back.

Once having done that, it was all surprisingly easy. He could just reach the first branch, and from there upwards the other branches went almost like a great spiral staircase, only getting thinner and thinner towards the top.

Up and up Sprout climbed. He could feel the whole tree swaying in the breeze, the higher he went. Once he looked down and caught a glimpse of Market, a red spot far below, through the fanned-out layers of dark needles. This quick look made him feel very giddy, so he scrambled on upwards without any more turning around. Suddenly, he found there was nothing up above him but the sky. No more tree; just a thin, swaying top branch with two tufts of pines and a fork in the middle where he could sit astride. He had never been so high up in his life. He thought how surprised the birds must be to see him there. But he was much more interested in how everybody else would *not* see him. It was the best hiding place of all. He knew it would be.

He began to eat the peanut-butter sandwiches. He thought of poor Market, far down below, not having any. But, without a trunk, how could he? Sprout was too miserable about that trunk to do anything but just sit there and sway and go on eating.

He finished the sandwiches and was on his second cookie when he heard them call. Of course, he took no notice. They sounded a long way away. He could hear the wind and himself crunching more loudly than those little voices. But then they came nearer, and he thought he heard someone say "Look!"

He crunched steadily on. They would never see him, however hard they looked. From underneath, the evergreen was dark and solid. He had been surprised, as he climbed, to find so many spaces and so much light. But those people down below would not know that. All they would see would be long pine needles.

The voices seemed to have stopped. He supposed they had gone back to their clay or something. He thought of them all cooped up in that lunchroom, while he sat here with a view of all the gardens for miles around. He could see the triangle where Miss Poddington's rabbit hutches were. It looked tiny. Then suddenly, nearer, down on the lawn, he saw Graham. He was walking backward, away from the tree, with his face turned up and his mouth open. He stopped. His eyes were frowned into slits against the sun, but he seemed to be looking straight at Sprout. Sprout sat quite still, but he felt the wind twirling the bit of hair on the top of his head.

"There he is, there he is!" shouted Graham, and pointed. Sprout saw some other figures running into sight on that piece of lawn. He ducked.

In the next second, the world was nothing but black branches and the grass flying up towards his head.

He didn't know how much later it was when he said, "Why am I going out of this door?" He only knew that he thought he saw the black-and-white-tiled floor and two ferns of Miss Poddington's front entrance; but it was all sideways, as if he was lying flat.

"Ssh!" said a voice. He thought it was his mother's.

"His trunk—" he began, but that was all.

6

"Where's my hair?"

Sprout lay in bed with his head hurting very much indeed. The first thing he had wondered was why, so he had put his hand up to see. Instead of the usual thicket, he felt a flat piece of stuff, smooth and stretched. Touching it, even with the tips of his fingers, made the pain worse, so did turning his head; so he just lay and waited.

"Ssh, dear," said his mother—this time he was sure of the voice—"lie quite still."

"I am," said Sprout. "But there's something funny on my head."

"It's all right, don't talk. The doctor will be coming to see you soon."

Sprout thought his mother sounded very strange and far away. He rolled his eyes around to make sure that she was there. Yes, it was her all right. She looked a rather queer color, but the same shape and with the same sweater on. It was his own same bed too, he realized slowly, but there was something the matter with the light. He rolled his eyes in the other direction and saw that the curtains were drawn. Outside, it looked as if it was still sunny.

"Is it early in the morning?" he asked.

"No," said his mother, "it's the afternoon, nearly time to feed Tilly. Now you mustn't talk anymore—"

"Why am I in bed?" demanded Sprout. "I don't go to bed before Tilly!" He tried to sit up, but his head made him flop back flat.

"Ssh! Today you have to," his mother said. "I imagine you've forgotten, but you had a very nasty fall. You even had to go to the hospital," she added, "and have your head stitched up."

"Stitched up?" said Sprout. "With a needle?"

"Ssh! Just lie still, and it'll soon be better."

Sprout touched the top of his head again. "That's not stitches," he said. "They've just stuck a patch on."

"That's the dressing," his mother told him, "and you mustn't touch it."

The curtain lifted in the breeze, and Sprout caught a glimpse of the trees outside the bedroom window. Suddenly he remembered.

"Where's Market?" he said loudly, and this time he really did sit up.

"It's all right," his mother soothed him, and bent forward to make him lie down again.

"It's not," he said. "His trunk broke off. I left it on the grass. Where is he?"

"Now do lie down. Really, Sprout, you must."

"I want to see Market."

"All right, dear, but—"

"Now!" said Sprout, and his head hurt so much that he couldn't help tears coming into his eyes.

"Very well, you shall see him now. I'll go and get him, but only if you promise to lie down and keep quite still—please!" His mother sounded very flustered and anxious. He hoped there wasn't anything worse the matter with Market.

"He hasn't broken anything else, has he?" he asked.

"No. Now don't move." And she went away.

The next morning, the doctor was surprised to find a large red elephant by the bed. He was even more surprised when he looked at Market's face.

"That's a funny elephant," he said. "What happened to his trunk?"

He was a doctor who always came straight to the

point, like Sprout. But he was worried when Sprout began to sit up and struggle with his pillows.

"What's up?" he said. "Not comfortable? Pillows feel a bit lumpy? I imagine they would, after you've had a bang like that."

"Here it is," said Sprout, and dragged Market's trunk out from under the bottom pillow. "I'm keeping it safe for him."

"I see," said the doctor. He examined the trunk carefully. "It seems to have been a clean break," he said. "Just a simple fracture."

"Does that mean it can be mended?" Sprout looked brighter than he had looked since Market hit the lawn mower.

"I should think a bit of plaster of paris might do the trick," said the doctor. "Now let's have a look at you, shall we?"

But Sprout wasn't really at all interested in this. He let the doctor feel his pulse and take his temperature, but he didn't listen to what his mother and the doctor were murmuring afterward. He heard a few words like "Lucky escape" and "A miracle" and "Twenty feet at least"; then he decided that they were talking too much about things that didn't matter, and not enough about things that did.

"Plaster of what, did you say?" he asked the doctor.

"Eh? Oh, paris. Plaster of paris. I'll write you out a prescription for it, shall I?"

The doctor had just scribbled something on a slip of
paper which he had given to Sprout's mother. Now,
he took another slip and wrote on it for Sprout. He
made him give Market's name, then he left that piece
of paper under the pillow with the trunk and said
"Keep it till you're up and about again. You can get it
at the hardware store."

Sprout couldn't read what was on the paper, but he
thought the doctor was a very sensible man, so much
so that he really listened when he was told again that
he must lie quite still.

"You do that, and I'll look in again in a few days'
time," said the doctor.

For two whole days, Sprout lay as still as a rock.

On the third day, his head had stopped hurting, and he sat up and said "I want to go and get that stuff for Market."

He was rather annoyed when his mother said he must wait. But she let him sit up and brought him hot buttered toast, two cupcakes, and lemon meringue pie for tea.

"I tried to get an elephant cake," she said, "but they don't make them."

"I wouldn't have eaten an elephant," said Sprout. He looked quite shocked. Then he saw something else on the corner of the tray.

"What's that?"

"Well, you can see. It's a bunch of violets."

"Oh."

"Aren't they nice? Guess who they're from!"

Sprout thought. "You," he said.

"No. Albina Chad!"

Sprout thought again. "Is it Tuesday?" he asked.

"No, they heard you were ill, and they came up especially. Wasn't that kind?"

"Yes, but I'm not sick now," said Sprout. "When can we get Market's stuff?"

At last the doctor came again and said Sprout could go out. They had gotten his tricycle back from the candy store, so with the flat white dressing still on the top of his head he rode slowly along to the hardware store.

Plaster of paris, which the doctor had written down on the slip of paper, turned out to be just a dry white powder, which the hardware-store man shoveled into a brown paper bag with a small metal scoop. He explained that you had to mix it up with water. Sprout thought this sounded interesting, and he rode back quite quickly, with the bag in the tricycle basket. He had not taken any of the other elephants. Until Market was mended, it didn't seem fair for them to go out.

His father helped him to mix up the powder. Then, they put some of it on Market's snout, some on his trunk, and pressed the two together until the paste leaked out at the sides.

"You'll have to hold it until it sets," his father said.

"How long?" asked Sprout. "Will somebody bring me my supper?" He was sitting on the floor in the shed. Then, to his great surprise, he felt the plaster getting hard already.

"It's quite quick," his father told him. "We'd better smooth it off a bit around the edges."

He took a piece of wet rag and started to rub it around Market's trunk. But the plaster had set too much to be quite smoothed off.

"There's a bump," said Sprout. "He looks as if he's got a whole doughnut stuck around his trunk."

"I think he always will," his father said. "But it might break again if we try to chip it."

"Don't let's do that, then," said Sprout quickly. "Anyway, maybe it'll be stronger than ever."

"I wouldn't be too sure," his father warned him. "You know, when things get broken, they're apt to break in the same place again." He dreaded what might happen if Market had any more accidents. It was better to let Sprout know the truth.

Sprout gazed at Market's trunk. "D'you mean it's weak," he asked, "as well as bumpy?"

"I'm only saying it might be. You'll just have to take care of him. We'll give him a little red paint on that joint."

"One thing," said Sprout slowly, "one thing I'll do is I'll never take him to school again."

"That's not a bad idea," said his father. But he didn't think it was such a good one when Sprout went on, even more slowly and firmly:

"I'll stay with him here. I'll stay with him all the time."

"Anyway, he *can't* go back to school yet," said his mother. "He hasn't even had his stitches out."

When she took Sprout to the hospital to have this done, he was very much surprised. First, because it was so quick: Not at all like when his mother had had to undo a seam to let out his jeans. Second, because of what he felt when he touched the top of his head: A bare patch.

"My hair *has* gone!" he said.

"Only a little bit," said his mother. "They had to shave that off to sew you up." But there were tears in her eyes: For the first time since he was born, Sprout had no sprout.

"I know what," said his father that night, "we'll all go to the zoo." He felt that Sprout's mother needed a break after all the anxiety, and he remembered that it was because of their not going that Tuesday, that Sprout had done what he had done. His father didn't want any more trouble.

"We'll have no peace until he's been there," he said.

Not that Sprout was being any particular trouble at the moment. His hair didn't worry him at all. He didn't give it another thought. All he worried about was looking after Market.

"When you say we'll all go," said his mother, "do you mean Tilly, too?"

"I don't see why not," his father said. "We can get the carriage in the car."

When they told Sprout, of course the first thing he said was "Can I take Market?"

No, they told him. Then, to avoid any argument, they pointed out that if Market had had an accident at school, he might have a much worse one in the car or at the zoo. Sprout saw their point.

"Well, can Albina come, then?" he said.

"Albina?" His father was surprised. But his mother thought it was very nice of Sprout. He had been grateful for those violets, after all.

"She's afraid of elephants," said Sprout. "I'll show her I'm not. I might even make her not be, too." He had forgotten the violets, but he did remember that it was because of Albina that he had gotten Market.

So on Saturday morning they went. Sprout sat in the front of the car with a huge bag of buns on his knee. Albina sat in the back with his mother and Tilly

and the carriage. His father had been going to fasten
that to the roof-rack, but Albina was so small that
there was plenty of room. She was completely silent
again. No one would ever have known that she could
tell a junk-shop man what she thought of him.

Sprout was silent too when at last—at long last—he
saw the real elephants. He saw three of them: two
were behind bars, curling their trunks through for
peanuts; the third was out on the path, with a line in
front of it.

"You'll have to stand there if you want a ride," said
his father.

Sprout stood, but not in line. He just stood looking
at the elephant's enormous wrinkled feet. Then, he
walked around and looked at its tail. Then, he went to
the other end and stared up at its great peaceful face.
Halfway up the face were eyes. He stood and looked
at these for a long time. What was more, he was sure
they were looking at him. They weren't so much
peaceful as beadily wide-awake, and they looked as if
they had kept wide-awake for many years. They had
little eyelashes and, far above them, marks like surprised, friendly eyebrows that had seen a joke. Of
course there were no eyebrows—just vague dents in
the thousands of crisscross creases of gray skin—but
the joke was there. Sprout felt that he shared it,
whatever it was. Slowly he grinned at the elephant,

and slowly, with even more creases in its skin, it smiled back. Other people might not have seen this, but Sprout did.

"Come on, get in line," said his father, "or we'll be here all day."

Sprout hoped they would be. He thought that was what they had come for, anyway. But he allowed himself to be nudged into a line of other children of all sizes and shapes, from a very small fat girl in frills to a very tall thin boy eating a banana.

"Come on," said Sprout to Albina. But she hung back.

Sprout noticed that quite a number of children were climbing up to have rides all at once. He was a little disappointed about this because he had imagined himself sitting on an elephant all alone. But this elephant itself was so wonderful that it didn't matter; it would even be a good thing, he thought, if Albina came on with him, so that he could sit in front of her and show her how silly it was to be afraid.

"Aren't you coming?" he asked her. But, just at that moment, the elephant, who had been watching everything, whipped its trunk around and removed the tall thin boy's banana.

"Hey," said the boy. "He ate it!"

Sprout roared with laughter. He doubled up and tottered sideways, and tears poured down his face. When he laughed, he really did laugh.

But the tall boy didn't, nor did Albina. In fact, the boy was so annoyed at everyone else's grins that he left the line and walked off, which put Sprout in the front place but one. As for Albina, she just looked more scared of elephants than ever.

"I don't want to," she said when Sprout's mother encouraged her to join him in the line. "It might eat my new hat." She was wearing a green and white knitted cap with a scarf to match. Mrs. Chad had only finished knitting them the night before, and Albina knew what a scolding she would get if anything happened to them.

"It wouldn't," said a voice in front of Sprout. "They don't eat hats."

Sprout looked to see where the voice had come from, but it was already halfway up the small ladder that led to the elephant's back.

"All right, one more," said the keeper who was in charge of the rides.

And a moment later, Sprout was actually sitting on the elephant.

"He was lucky," said his father. "If that boy with the banana hadn't gone away, he would have had to wait another half hour."

Albina thought she was lucky too; she had gotten out of it. If Sprout had been the first in the next lot, they would have tried again to make her go. She realized that. Now she could stand comfortably down below, holding on to Tilly's carriage. That was what she much preferred to do.

Sprout looked down at them all. He could hardly believe that he was here at last.

"You're squashing me," said the voice in front of him. It looked around. Sprout saw that it belonged to a very tiny boy with dark hair and a rather yellow face. He stared hard. He knew he had seen this boy somewhere before.

"I know!" he said. "You were in our candy store!" And then he remembered that he had also seen this boy going into one of the big apartment houses at the bottom of their road.

"So were you in *our* candy store!" said the boy. And then he suddenly made a loud noise that sounded like "Hmit!"

"What did you say?" asked Sprout.

"Hmit!" said the boy. "Why doesn't he sit down?"

"Who?"

"The elephant. That's what they said to them in Burma when they wanted them to sit down. Hmit! And they did."

"What, sit down?"

"Yes. HMIT!" the boy shouted more loudly, but nothing happened, except that all the other children in front looked around.

"If this one did, we should all fall off," said Sprout. The keeper, anyway, was just getting the elephant to walk along. Sprout was too much interested and excited to think about his parents and Tilly and Albina. He just sat bolt upright.

"Tah!" said the boy in front of him suddenly.

"That's what babies say," Sprout remarked. "I say thank you."

"Tah means stand up. It's an elephant word," said the boy.

Sprout rode on in silence for a moment.

"How do you know?" he asked.

"In Burma they say it."

"What's Burma?"

"Where I was before I came here."

"Are there a lot of elephants there?"

"Hundreds and hundreds."

Sprout stared at the boy with wonder and envy. This was the first other person he had ever met who really seemed to know what was worth knowing. Yet he was such a small boy, about half Sprout's size.

"I've got an elephant at home," said Sprout, to keep his own end up. "But he couldn't come here because he's got a weak trunk."

"Do you sing to him?"

"No. Why?"

"They sing to them to make them come. And play on pipes. I've got a pipe, I brought it back with me."

"Oh." Sprout was getting more and more envious,

but he wanted to hear more, too. "Would you like to come to tea?" he asked.

"When?"

"Tomorrow. My elephant's red; he's called Market. What's the matter with his trunk is, he broke it at school. But we got some stuff—"

"Oh, do you go to school?" The small boy's face suddenly lit up, less yellow and more pinkish. He turned around and stared at Sprout.

"Yes. Well, I did go," Sprout said carefully. "I've stopped now." He was thinking of Market.

"Real school?" the boy gasped. "With desks?"

"Well, tables," said Sprout. "It's Miss Poddington's."

"Oh, you are lucky!"

Sprout looked at the boy with great surprise. "Lucky?"

"I wish I went to school. I do wish I did."

"Well, why don't you?"

"I don't like our apartment. There's nobody to play with, and I have to be quiet all the time because of the old lady underneath. Anyway, if you can go to school, why can't I?"

Sprout thought about this. "All right," he said, "you come." He beamed comfortably, as if it were all settled—just as he had beamed at the man with the junk-shop truck. "You come to Miss Poddington's.

Instead of Market. Then I'll go again, too. But you have to bring your own cookies," he added. "They only give you milk, and not much, either."

The elephant swung around, lurching back to the place on the path where a new line had formed.

"Sprout seems to have made a friend," remarked his father. He looked up and saw the two boys talking solemnly.

"Trust him to do that on top of an elephant," his mother smiled.

"Oh well, I dare say he'll get over his elephants. I imagine he's gotten over that hiding business, anyway. After what happened."

His mother said nothing. Albina Chad stood and waved.

"Seems funny, though," his father said, "seeing him without that old sprout of hair on top."

His mother looked up at the pink face on the back of the elephant.

"It'll grow again," she said.